The Learning Support Department
Aster School

CW00692762

The Learning Support Department
Aster School

For Michael

First Published in Great Britain in 1989 by Hutchinson Children's Books
An imprint of Century Hutchinson Ltd
Brookmount House, 62-65 Chandos Place,
Covent Garden, London WC2N 4NW

Century Hutchinson Australia (Pty) Ltd
20 Alfred Street, Milsons Point, Sydney NSW 2061

Century Hutchinson New Zealand Limited
32-34 View Road, PO Box 40-086, Glenfield, Auckland 10

Century Hutchinson South Africa (Pty) Ltd
PO Box 337, Bergvlei 2012, South Africa

Designed by ACE Ltd
Set in Madison Roman by The Graphic Unit, London

Printed and bound in Belgium by
Proost International Book Production

British Library Cataloguing in Publication Data

Pike, Carol.
   The nutty queen.
   I. Title.
   821'914   [J]

ISBN 0-09-173795-8

Carol Pike

The Nutty Queen

HUTCHINSON
London Sydney Auckland Johannesburg

The Nutty Queen she bought a boat,
And sailed across the sea.
'I've left the King to see the world.
I'll not be back for tea.'

She landed on the Loopee Shores,
A sports day was in swing.
She bet some moles she'd win at bowls,
But never scored a thing!

She slept a night, and then sailed on,
Bound for the Isle of Cats.
She took some frocks and yellow socks,
And a pile of fancy hats.

She bade the pussies all farewell,
Sailed to the Land of Peas,
And there she tucked up all her skirts,
And swung amongst the trees.

The Queen sailed on, for three whole days,
To find excitement new,
She ventured on an ancient land,
Where dozy dodos flew.

The Queen tied up the yellow boat
And, much to her delight,
She met a charming dinosaur,
They waltzed throughout the night.

By rising sun, the Queen moved on,
Through miles of glistening sand,
For she'd been told the Blushing Fish
Lived east, across the land.

The Blushing Fish told many tales
At which the Queen did laugh.
They drank champagne with buttered toast,
Whilst sitting in the bath.

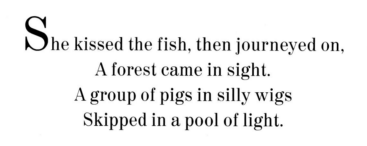

She kissed the fish, then journeyed on,
A forest came in sight.
A group of pigs in silly wigs
Skipped in a pool of light.

The Queen sat down to watch the fun,
Joined by some circus bears.
They played backgammon, ate smoked salmon,
Honey and pickled pears.

A year from home, and still she roamed.
She hopped from shore to shore,
And when she thought she'd seen the world,
She went around once more!

The Queen at last sailed homeward bound,
The King was full of glee.
A cake was made, the table laid.
They both sat down to tea!